NOTE TO PARENTS

This well known fairytale has been specially written and adapted for 'first readers', that is, for children who are just beginning to read by themselves. However, for those not yet able to read, then why not read this story aloud to your child, pointing to the words and talking about the pictures? There is a word list at the back of the book which identifies difficult words and explains their meaning in the context of the story.

Heidi

retold by Brenda Apsley
illustrated by Gill Guile

Once there was a little girl
called Heidi.
When her parents died Heidi was
sent to live with her aunt.

One day Heidi's aunt said,
"I am taking you to stay with
your grandfather.
It is his turn to look after you."
Heidi's grandfather lived alone
in a hut in the mountains.

When they found him he was sitting
on a bench outside his hut.
He did not want Heidi to stay with
him, but he said, "Come inside."

Inside, Heidi climbed up into a room
where Grandfather kept hay.
From a little window she could see
far across the tops of the mountains.
"I'll sleep here," said Heidi.

Peter the goatherd came to the hut.
Every morning he took the goats up
on to the mountain to feed.
Every evening he brought them
down again.

"This white goat is called
Little Swan," said Grandfather.
"The brown one is Little Bear."
He milked Little Swan and gave
Heidi a bowl of milk for supper.
Then she went to bed.

Next morning, Peter came to take
Little Bear and Little Swan
up to the mountain.
"Would you like to go with him?"
asked Grandfather.
"Oh yes!" said Heidi.

Heidi spent many happy hours
with Peter and the goats.
She learned all their names.
"But Little Bear and Little Swan
are the prettiest," said Heidi.

Then the snow came.
Now Peter did not take the goats
to the mountain.
One day he called to see Heidi.
"Will you come to my house?
Granny wants to meet you," he said.

Peter's grandmother was blind.
She asked Heidi to tell her
all about her life on the mountain.
Later, Peter returned from school.
He told them how he was learning
to read.

Granny said she had a book of hymns
she had not heard for many years.
"I hope that one day Peter will
read them to me," she said.

One day Heidi's aunt came to visit.
"I have a surprise," she said.
"A rich family in the city
want you to live with them.
They have a daughter who is ill.
Her name is Clara.
You will be her friend."

Heidi did not want to go.
"But you'll learn to read and write,"
said her aunt, "and you can bring
back presents for Grandfather,
Peter and Granny."
So Heidi set off for the city.

Clara's teacher asked Heidi,
"What books have you read?"
"I can't read," said Heidi.
"How shocking!" said the teacher.

Heidi was very unhappy.
She missed Grandfather so much.
Heidi could only see walls, rooftops
and chimneys from her window.
There were no mountains here
in the city.

There were rules for everything —
for going to bed and getting up,
for going out and coming in, for
opening doors and shutting windows.
"I wish I was back on the mountain
with Grandfather," sighed Heidi.

Lessons began next morning, but
soon the teacher heard a loud crash.
Heidi had knocked the table over.
Her books fell on to the floor.
"It's that terrible child!"
said the teacher.

Clara said, "It wasn't Heidi's fault.
She thought she heard the wind in the
fir trees and rushed to see them."
"Fir trees!" said the teacher.
"What nonsense!"

Heidi grew to love Clara,
but still she was not happy.
She became pale and thin.
The doctor was sent for.
"Are you happy here?" he asked.
"People are kind," said Heidi.
"But I do miss my grandfather."

"Heidi is very homesick,"
the doctor said.
"You must not keep her here
any longer."
Clara was sad but her father
promised she could visit Heidi.

Next morning Heidi went back home,
up the mountain path.
Grandfather was so pleased to see her.
"I'm home," cried Heidi.

Heidi's grandfather did not speak,
but his eyes were wet with tears.
Very gently he took Heidi's hand,
and together they went into the hut.

Heidi visited Peter's granny in
the morning.
"I can read now," she said.
And Granny listened as Heidi read
from the old hymn book.

Heidi was made even happier
when Clara came to stay.
Each morning, Grandfather carried
Clara up the mountain.
There she spent many happy hours
with Peter, the goats, and Heidi.

New words

Did you see a lot of new words in the story? Here is a list of some hard words from the story, and what they mean.

city
a big town

goatherd
someone who looks after goats

homesick
to feel sad because you miss your home

hymn
a song that you sing to God

mountain
a very big hill

prettiest
the best looking

promise
to say something will happen